The Adventures of
OOK AND GLUK
KUNG-FU CAVEMEN FROM THE FUTURE

by George Beard and ... ...

Scholastic Inc.

New York Toronto London Auckland Sydney
Mexico City New Delhi Hong Kong Caveland, Ohio

For Connor Mancini

This book is being published simultaneously in hardcover by the Blue Sky Press.

ISBN 978-0-545-38577-0 (Trade) / ISBN 978-0-545-19576-8 (BC)

Be sure to check out Dav Pilkey's Extra-Crunchy Web Site O' Fun at www.pilkey.com.

27 26   19 20/0

Printed in the United States of America   40
First printing, August 2010

A SCIENTIFIC DISCLAIMER

By

Professor Gaylord M. Sneedly

The book you hold in your hands contains many scientific errors and stuff.

For example, dinosaurs and cavemen did not live at the same time. Dinosaurs lived more than 64 million years BEFORE cavemen.

And I should know! In 2003, I was the recipient of The Most Brilliantest Science Guy of the Whole Wide World Award.

So there!

Professor Gaylord M. Sneedly

A SCieNTiFic DiSCLAiMER DiSCLAiMER

BY George and Harold

SCieNTists Think They Know every-thing!

BuT They dont!

They Just make guesses based on evidense Theyv'e already discovered.

I call my guesses "Theries" so They sound important!

← "Genius"

BuT Theres all kinds of NEW evidense discovered every day!

So the "TRuTH" is alwaYs changing!

Forchenately, we have a Time machine.

Purple Potty Co.

We've Been To The Future and the Past!

So we discovered Lots of evidence That scientists dont Know About... YET!!!

For exampel: Some dinosaurs Did Live The same Time as cavemen!

Hey

What UP?

But scientists wont discover That until The year 2073!

So if your Looking for guesses, There are plenty of Science books To choose From.

The Origin OF Guesses

a Brief history of guesses

Or you can Read The Worlds First Book Based on SCIENCE FACTS!!!

CHAPTERS

1. Meet Ook and Gluk.......7

2. The Goppernoppers Strike Back...41

3. Training Time..........71

4. The Heros Jerney....95

5. The Terror of The ~~Mec~~
Mechasaurs........123

6. Two Wongs dont make
it right...........145

Epalog...........166

The Adventures of OOK and GLUK

KUNG-FU CAVEMEN FROM THE FUTURE

CHAPTER 1
Meet OOK and GLUK

This is Ook Schadowski and Gluk Jones. Ook is the kid on the left with the missing tooth and the stringy haircut. Gluk is the kid on the right with the Lepard-spots and the afro.

remember that now!

Ook and Gluk lived way back in the year 500,001 B.C. in a village called Caveland, Ohio.

welkum to caveland

OOK and GLUK were best friends.

They had Been having Awesome Adventures Together ever Sinse They were cave Babys.

Ha-Ha   PBBBT   Grrr

Once When they were 3, they went over a waterfal on a Log.

Weeeeee

OK...

OW! me Bwoke MY TOOF!

Another time when they were 7, they almost got ate up by Mog-Mog: The fearsest dinosaur in Caveland.

And once they even traveled to the future, learned Kung-Fu, and saved there whole villege from evil robots and time-traveling weirdos!

But before we can tell you that story, we have to tell you

THIS STORY

This is BiG cheif Goppernopper.

He was the Ruler of Caveland and He hated Ook and Gluk.

Grrrr

Every time chief Goppernopper tried to be a big shot, Ook and Gluk always ruined it!

clank clank

Look at me! Me invented wheel!

SHOOM

Look at me! me created spear!

SNAP

BOOM

Look at me! me Discovered **FiRE!**

ZOOOOOOM

Those two Kids driving me CRAZY! Me need to sit on throne and relax!

What the?

OOK WUZ HERE

GLUK TOO

GARDS!!

Here we are, cheif Grasshopper.

My Names Not Grass-Hopper, Its Goppern-opper!!! Jeez, How many times me got to Tell you?

We Sorry, Chief Gobstopper.

14

One hour Later, They arived at Ooks and Glukses caves.

oh, and "Buck"

Dont For-ger "Luck"

SCHAD-OWSKI

JONES

ALRight You dumb Kids Your under arest !!!

When Ooks Sister, Gak, heard The Comosh-en, she pleeded with chief Goppernopper.

aw have mercy and stuff!

Ooh, Hubba Hubba! Me Think mes in Love!

Ew Gross.

Will you mary me?

No way ya dumb head

16

Psst! me no Think she Like you, Chief Gumwrapper.

It's "GOB STOPPER" ...I mean "GOPPER-Nopper", you idiot! Now Youv'e got me doing it !!!

ZONG

Listen Bub, You Better mary me Tomorow, or me gonna throw Uck and Gluk in the slammer!

Hims Name not Uck, it "Ook".

ryme with "duke"

LETS GO!

Boo Hoo Hoo! Now me gotta mary That Jerk!

and "spook" and "Kook"

17

18

Me think we made new Freinds!

me too.

Hey, MaYBe new Freinds can help sister, Gak!

Yeah!

Lets Go!

Meanwhile back in Caveland, a wedding is happenning

Do you, chief GOOBERpicker, take this—

Thats GOPpernopper!!

oh yeah. Do you take Gak to be cave wife?

me Do!

And do you, Gak, Take cheif uh... um...

Do you take this little guy over here to Be Cave husbend?

No way Hozãy!

BOOM BOOM BOOM BOOM

CRASH!

We OBJECK!!!

Me Too!

OK Baby Mog-Mog. see That guy down There With Pointy nose?

Sik-em!

WARNING

The FoLowing seckshon conTains graphic violins and may not be suitible for sensative grownups and Other people who arent very fun.

FLIP-O-RAMA

Here's How it Works!!!

STEP 1
Plase your Left hand inside the dotted Lines marked "Left Hand HERE." Hold the Book open FLAT.

STEP 2
GRASP the Right-hand Page with YOUR RIGHT Thumb and index finGER (inside the dotted Lines marked "RIGHT THuMB HERE").

STEP 3
Now Quickly FLiP the Right-hand Page back and FOURTH Until the Pitcher apears to Be Animated!

(For extra fun, try adding your own Sound afecks)

FLIP-O-RAMA #1

(Pages **37** and **39**)

Remember, flip Only page **37**. While you are fliping, be shure you can See the Pitcher On Page **37** And the one on page **39**.

IF you Flip Quickly, the two pitchers WiLL Start to Look Like ONE animated pitcher.

Dont Forget to add your own Sound Afecks.

Left Hand Here

Do the Bite Thing

right thumb Here

Do the Bite thing

OW! me hate you guys!

aw, that too bad.

Me sick of Being your Cheif. Me Quit!!

Good! You Lousy cheif anyways!

Bye Bye now.

come on, GARds!

Me going to get revenge on Ook and Gluk one day. And that goes for Gake, Too!

Her name not Gake. It "GAK".

Ryme with tack.

CHAPTER 2

5 days later, X-chief Goppernopper was about to discover a starteling discovery.

44

ALL This "Crazy stuff" is really just machines from the future.

no way!

Way! My Company has a Time Machine. We use it to steal stuff.

Awesome! Stealing rules!

I Know. This Time machine Lets us pillege the earth and crush anybody who stands in our way!!!

HAW! HAW! Evil give me warm feeling!

500,001 B.C.

Check this out: Right Now were in the year 500,001 B.C. But if you step through this portal...

...You will end up in the year 2222 AD. This is where Im from. Welcome to the Headquarters of Goppernopper Enterprises.

Here, have a complamentery coffey mug and mousepad.

awesome.

But me no understand how come you need Time Portal?

We bring it all back to modern times and sell it for huge profits! Cheers!

Hmmm. What you doing seem Reckless and iresponsible! Me Love it!!!

ZAP

OIL

G CAVEMAN WATER only $9.99

G CAVEMAN WATER only $9.99

You Know, Gramps, I Like the way you think! Howd you Like to work for me?

OK

Great! Your Hired! we wont rest until we have stolen all The trees, oil, and water from the past!

How you like some Slaves, too?

Slaves?

Yeah. Me know where whole village of cavemen Live.

Awesome! HAW! HAW! Haw!

48

50

Left hand
Here

Bunches-o-Punches!

RIGHT THUMB Here

53

Bunches-o-Punches!

The citizins of Caveland marched for days until They finally came to The Time Portal.

OK, Slaves! Grab a Shovel and start diggin!!!

SOON...

man, me hate being slave.

me too.

HEY!!!

These are 2 Troublemakers me telled you About. Me think They be perfect for Torcher expariments!

Hmmm. This sounds like fun!

57

welcome to Gopper-nopper Tower --- my World headquarders and Torcher center.™

60

STOP THEM!

meanwile...

EXIT

soon our heros found themselfes running for their lifes in a strange futuristic city from the future.

Here they come!

Stop or me shoot!

me too!

Quick hide behind this sign.

our

62

scratch
scratch

They went that-a-way!

You may hide in my school if you like.

Gee Thanks.

trash

MASTER WONG'S School of KUNG-FU

That night, Master Wong's daughter, Lan, cooked a big dinner. Ook and Gluk told them everything that happend.

What we do now?

Hmmm...

You must stay ~~here~~ here and Learn the ways of Kung-Fu.

Then when you are ready, Perhapse you can help your family and freinds.

But how? Goppernopper company so big, we just small kids.

There is no Big. No small.

huh?

Look at baby dinosaur. Is she big or small?

That easy. She small.

Lets ask the same queshtion to this Ladybug.

Yo man, she Big!

69

Big and small are oposites. How can both be true at the same Time?

Big and small have no real meaning. Only in your mind.

Therefore you must Look Beyond the surfise to see what is real. In yourselfs and in others.

Boy, philosofy make my brain hurt.

Yep. That'll happen.

Chapter 3

Training Time

The next Day

Hey whats your pet dinosaurs name anyway?

Ummm... She no really have name, me guess.

Well Im going To call her Lily cuz Lilies are my faverite flowers.

OK

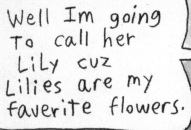

Today we begin your instruckshon. What is it you wish to Learn?

Me want to Learn how to Kick butt.

me too.

Those who Kick butt are weak. For Violens has no mind.

aw man!

If you truley want to set things right, you must walk the Path of Peace.

Here are two white Belts. they are simbels of your dedicashen To your Training

cool.

When can we learn to use spears and Knifes and stuff?

Those who Truley desire peace must not carry weapons.

For the simple Knife that cuts Bread also cuts Flesh.

The Lowley axe That chops wood also chops bones.

chop!

and the commen spear that Kills fish also Kills man.

Yet a man of peace must not be weak.

So every finger must become a dagger...

snap

Chop

...every open hand an axe...

...and every arm a spear.

CRACK

When can we learn nun-chucks?

Slap

The Best fighters do not show off thier anger.

The wisest warrior wins without a battle.

The flexeble willow Tree does not fight against the Storm --- yet it survives.

clay may be shaped into a bowl...

and a house may be formed from logs...

But it is the spaces within which make these things usefull.

So we must listen for the spaces within us.

SPLISH

PLip

SPLASH

Ook and Gluk studied math, sciense, grammer, speling and chemistry.

They also studied important Things, too.

music and art are like eating and breathing.

One cannot truely live without them.

Even when Ook and Gluk wern't studying, they were still learning.

Your minds are free to follow theyr'e own paths. They may soar to the heavens or rot in a prisen. Its up to you!

He who conquers his own mind is the greatest warrier.

The mind is stronger than the flesh. It can defeat any oponent, no matter how strong.

Ook and Gluk practiced thier Kung-Fu every day.

Soon they got really good.

FLIP-O-RAMA 3

Left hand Here

Kung-Fu Fever

RIGHT
Thumb
Here

Kung-Fu Fever

Even Lily tried to learn the ways of Kung Fu --- but every time she spinned around, she threw up.

FLIP-O-RAMA 4

Left hand Here

Lily Loses Lunch!

RIGHT THUMB here

Lily Loses Lunch!

Many months passed, and finelly Ook and Gluk had trained for one year.

master wong, when we going to get new belts?

yeah. white belts not too cool anymore.

Master Wong thought for a long time then he asked Ook and Gluk a Queshtion.

Who is the greatest man?

Ummmm..

You?

no! No new belts for you.

aw, man!

Another whole year came and went. Again Ook and Gluk asked about the belts.

We want cool Black Belts!

What we have to do To get Black Belts?

Master Wong asked them the same Queshtion again.

Who is the greatest man?

Ummm

hmmm...

a King? The President?

no! No black belts for you.

Rats!

One year later, the same thing hapened.

Come on, Please?

Even purple belts be kind of cool.

seeds

Peas

again Master wong asked the boys:

who is the greatest man?

me?

me too?

No. No purple belts for you.

Bummer.

Years came and went, and Ook and Gluk grew bigger and stronger all the time.

even Ooks missing tooth grew back in.

me Look awesome!

in your dreams!

But in all that time, they never fig-yured out who the greatest man was.

our ansesters?

no.

The Pope?

no.

Teachers?

no.

a artist?

no.

敬

Popeye?

no.

a woman?

no.

Lily didn't get much bigger, and she never Learned to spin around without barfing, either.

Dad, get the mop!

CHAPTER 4
The Heros Jerney

Seven years had come and gone. In that time, Ook and Gluk had grown into men.

The time now come for us to fase us's destiny.

O.K.

Lets go.

Oh Ook, Be carefull!!! Dont get hurT!!! I couldent Bear it if anything bad happened to you!!

Hey what about us?

Oh yeah. You too.

Thank you Master Wong. We will do our best to save village and defeet evil Goppernoppers.

may you have suckesss on your Jerney.

Oh, by way, we finelly think we figured out who greatest man is.

MAST
Sc
Ku

and who might that be?

nobody.

MASTER
Scho
Ku

Yes. That is corect.

Titles and trophies have no value to the man who is at peace with himself.

True greatness is anonamus. Therefore the greatest man is nobody.

umm... OK...

Well... me guess we better be—

Hey, you dropped something.

WOAH!!! Black Belts!

Ook, Gluk, and Lily walked threw the poluted city toward Goppernopper Enterprises.

These new Black Belts really cool... but me still a little woried.

Remember what Master Wong say: "Dont...umm...Dont be scared and stuff."

But they got Lazer guns and Torcher machines

Master Wong say: "Brains is more awesome than other... umm... stuff. Brains can defeet even strongest enemy guys."

Master Wong talk better than you.

Yeah me know. Him have way with words.

Soon they reached there destinashon

Left hand Here

Ook's Rebuke!

RIGHT THUMB HERE

Ook's Rebuke!

Left Hand Here

GLUK Amuck!

Right thumb Here

GLUK Amuck!

We gotta get inside that bilding!!!

O.K.

CRASH!

Hey, your not alowed to do that!

I'm telling!

Ook, Gluk and Lily searched the strange hallways of Goppernopper Enterprises looking for the Time Portal.........

Polushen departmint

Torcher Room

Stealing Departmint

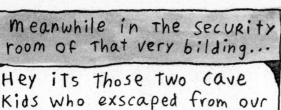

meanwhile in The security room of That very bilding...

well They wont exscape again!!!

Hey its those Two cave Kids who exscaped from our evil clutches seven years ago!!!

ecurity Moniter 2

RELEASE the kiLLER ROBots!!!

SMASH

BOOM BOOM BOOM Boom

CLICK

RRRR

KA CHUNK

BOING

OOK, you ok?

Me BWOKE TOOF Again.

113

The Killer Robots capchered our heros in thier crushing claws.

and only one thing stood in thier way.

NOT SO FAST!!!

You think you **can** just barge in here, bust up my Robots, and get away with it?

what the...???

WARNING:
The following scene may be too discusting for some viewers --- espeshelly for viewers who have just eaten watery oatmeal, corn chowder, or cream of mushroom soup.

FLIP-O-RAMA 7

Left hand Here

Regergitation
Animation

Right
thumb
here.

Regergitation
Animation

So Ook, Gluk, and Lily ran back through the time portal, unaware of the terror that awaited them.

CHAPTER 5

THE TERROR OF THE

MECHASAURS

When Ook, Gluk and Lily got back to prehistoric times, they dident even reckegnise the place.

The three friends searched the raveged land for thier fellow Cavelanders.

Soon they found them--- still enslaved.

Let my people go and stuff.

No way!!!

ZAP

POW WHAM CHOMP

me get computer savy in past seven years.

So me uploaded pictures of you into memory banks of mech-asaurs!

Me programed them to attack whenever they see your faces! HAW! HAW! Haw!

Sik 'em!

The mechasaurs chased Ook, Gluk, and Lily across the horizen...

... and followed them back to 2229 A.D.

130

Our three heros ran between the many warehouses and stockrooms.

Finelly they found a good place to hide.

133

The mechasaurs crushed each bilding almost as fast as our heros could paint.

But there was STILL one Big bilding That needed To be **CRUSHED**

Left hand here

Mechasaurus
Wrecks!

mechasaurus
wrecks!

With Goppernopper Enterprises in Flames and the mechasaurs destroyed, Ook and Gluk vowed to Rebild their world.

They started by sending chief Goppernopper and his evil workers back to the year 2229 AD.

aw, man!

now it time to find your mom!!!

But before They got a chanse, a paper airplane sailed Through the time portal.

Gluk unfolded the paper and read the horrible message.

atenchen Ook and Gluk,
I have capchered master Wong and his doughter. Give up now or They will be killed to death!
Sincerely yours,
J.P. Goppernopper

CHAPTER →6←

TWO WONGS DON'T MAKE IT RIGHT

147

They were easy to find and they'll be even easier to KILL !!!

WAIT!

LET them go and we do whatever you say!

OK. Its a dea BUT PUT Thes handcufs on first.

OK.

SOON

I know I promised To Let your freinds go, but I changed my mind. I'm going To kill all of you!

148

HAW! HAW! HAW!!!

How we ever going to get out of this?

remember your tra-ining my child.

Ook and Gluk closed thier eyes and tried to remember all the wise stuff that Master Wong had told them.

The mind is stronger than the flesh. It can defeat any oponent, no matter how strong.

Gopper-nopper Tower

The wizest warrior wins without a battle.

True greatness is anonamuss. There-fore the greatest man is...

Finelly, Ook and Gluk got a idea....

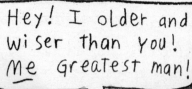

Your the Father of my Butt!!!

One day when me have Kids, me going to teach them some MANNERS!!!!!

You? Have Kids? HAH!!! Whose going to mary you? You look like a little salt shaker!

Maybe me teach YOU some manners!

You couldent teach a skunk to stink, you dumb old Caveman!!!

at Least me not wear wig!

153

Left hand
Here

The Pain Event!

RIGHT
THUMB
Here

The Pain Event!

If you no longer exist, then neether does your company.

everything you built or created is begining to disapear.

including our ropes and chains.

The world we once knew is being replased by a world without Goppernoppers.

SudenLy Ook and GLuK remembered something important.

The Time PoRTaL!!!

Our three Heros ran back To the time portal, which was also starting to disapear.

Quick! It almost Gone!!! Bye master Wong!!!

Bye Lan!

Bye

ZAP

master Wong turned and walked back home.

it was a Jerney he had walked many Times.

... but This Time was more like a dream

But somehow I feel like a part of them is still very near.

EPiLOG

502,223 years and 49 minutes earlier...

As the time portal slowly disapeared, the world began to change back to normel.

So OOK, GLUK, Lan and Lily started off on thier Long WALK to CaveLand.

and before too Long, They ran into a old friend.

Learn to Speak caveman Language!!!

CAVEMONICS

It Fun!

It easy!

it Annoy Grown-ups!

Lesson #1	Turn "I" into "Me"

Want to talk Like Caveman? First Rule: No more use Pronoun "I". Instead use "Me"

Lets Practise!

ENGLISH	CAVEMONICS
I Like candy.	= Me Like candy.
I play baseball.	= Me play baseball.
I am awesome.	= Me awesome.

171

LeSSon #2   Simplify

Drop any unnesessary informashon. Also, try to find simple replacements for words with more than two syLables.

Lets Practise

ENGLiSH		CAVeMONiCS
I dont care for anchovies on my Pizza.	=	Me no Like Little fishes.
I'm going to the LocaL Amusement Park today.	=	Me go to Barf ride Place.
I'd Like to eat at Applebees.	=	me go to Barf place.

LeSSon #3

Avoid contractions

Stay away from words like "dont," "cant" and "havent." Instead try to use the simplest form of the word as a replacement. In many cases, "no" will do just fine.

Lets Practise

ENGLiSH	CAVEMONICS
I cant spel very well.	= me no spel good.
I havent done my homework.	= me do homework. Dog eat it.
My Grandmother doesnt think this book belongs in The school Library.	= Grandma no fun.

Lesson # 4

Try say everything in "Present tense" Whenever you can!

Lets Practise

ENGLISH		CAVEMONICS
I was born on August 14th.	=	me born one day.
Yesterday I went swimming at The water park.	=	me catch Parasite infection day before now.
my annoying next-door-naybors are going to move away This weekend.	=	So Long, Suckas!

See more tips at WWW.PILKEY.COM

The Ook and Gluk Adventure Continues Online at WWW.PILKEY.COM and WWW.SCHOLASTIC.COM

Watch a film about how the book was made!

Cool!

Learn how to draw Ook, Gluk, Lily, the Mechasaurs, and MORE!

Free Downloads! Free Video Games!

Free!

Awesome!

Meet the "REAL" Lily!

About The Author and Illustrator

GEORGE BEARD (age 9³/₄) is the co-creator of Captain Underpants, Super Diaper Baby, Hairy Potty, and The Amazing Cow Lady.

In his spare time, George enjoys skateboarding, playing with his two cats, and making comic books with his best friend, Harold Hutchins.

For the past seven months, George has taken Kung-Fu lessons at Master Wong's School of Kung-Fu in Piqua, Ohio. George currently wears a green belt.

HAROLD HUTCHINS (age 10) is a fourth grader at Jerome Horwitz Elementary School. He has written and illustrated more than 30 comic books with his best friend, George Beard.

In his spare time, Harold enjoys skateboarding, drawing, watching movies, and chewing gum.

Harold takes classes at Master Wong's School of Kung-Fu. Recently, Harold earned the title of purple belt although he is keenly aware that it's "not about the belt."